Forgotten Reboot

Herobrine's Quest – Book No. 8

by Steve DeWinter

Disclaimer:

Summary

Walter explains to Larissa what is actually happening, and who she really is, while Andre is convinced to help protect the access point from his own brother at any cost.

Do you want the author of this book to visit your classroom?

Ask your teacher to contact Steve DeWinter at writer@stevedw.com to discuss having an author visit with your class using the power of the internet and a webcam.

Watch Steve and his son, the real Josh who inspired the Josh in this story, play games and have fun together on their YouTube Channel.

ODNT
OLD DOG NEW TRX
LET'S PLAY

https://www.youtube.com/c/odnttv

This book is a work of fiction. References to real people, events, establishments, organization, or locales are intended only to provide a sense of authenticity, and are used fictitiously. All other characters, and all incidents and dialogue, are drawn from the author's imagination and are not to be construed as real.

Ramblin' Prose Publishing

eBook Edition

ISBN-10: 1-61978-126-3

ISBN-13: 978-1-61978-126-9

Paperback Edition

ISBN-10: 1-61978-127-1

ISBN-13: 978-1-61978-127-6

Chapter 1

Larissa stood in the stark white space as she heard Walter speak to her from everywhere, and nowhere, at the same time.

"Let me show you why what we are doing is so important."

She watched as the white space around her shifted and filled in. First, it was just lines being drawn that slowly resembled objects, as if they were being drawn in midair. The lines of each item were in a precise gridded pattern.

Then space between the lines quickly filled in to reflect solid surfaces, yet everything was still a pale gray.

The next thing to happen was a blurry mesh of colors that started out as overlapping blobs that kept shifting into smaller blobs.

The resolution of the objects around her became sharper until she saw she was standing in the middle of a city unlike any she had ever seen before.

The buildings, while still made of a type of smooth stone, were taller than the tallest spire she had seen on the biggest castles. There were buildings that shined with a transparent material that reflected the other buildings around them.

There were so many tall buildings built close together, it was dizzying to even fathom who could have done something so wondrous.

Walter's voice broke the silence.

"This is the world as it is today."

She looked around her at the vast expanse of buildings.

"Where? I have never seen anything remotely like it."

"What you are seeing is an image of the real world."

"The real world? What does that mean?"

"I don't know how to say this to you other than by being direct. You are not real."

She frowned, looking around her, not sure which way she should be facing to talk with the disembodied voice.

"Not real?"

"Not in the way you are thinking."

"I feel real."

"You were designed to not know the difference between what is real and what is manufactured."

She shook her head. "I don't know who you are, but you can't convince me I'm not real."

"I don't have to convince you. You will convince yourself."

"What? How?"

"Look at your skin."

She lifted her arm to look at it and a gasp

of surprise escaped her lips. Her arm was its normal color; not green. She spun around and looked at her reflection in a nearby window.

Her face was also the correct color. She moved closer to the window and looked into her clear eyes. They were no longer bloodshot and red.

She ran her tongue along her teeth. The extended fangs were gone.

She smiled wide and turned her head back and forth as she inspected her normal teeth in the reflection of the window.

"This is a trick. The same magic you used to create this empty city, you are using on me to make me think I am no longer a zombie.

But you can't change the past."

"The past has already been changed. I am more worried about the future."

"What do you mean the past has been changed?"

"Before we discuss more, there is someone else who can convince you that I am not tricking you."

"Who?"

A new voice came from directly behind her. "Me."

She spun around, and her heart skipped a beat.

"Mother?"

Her mother, not the zombie version, but

her real mother before Herobrine had changed her, smiled. “Hello sweetheart.”

Larissa shook her head as tears formed in her eyes. “It can’t be you.”

Her mother smiled. “It is me. Walter brought me back.”

Larissa took a step backward. “What form of dark magic is this?”

Her mother took a step forward. “Not magic. Science. He reset my program.”

“You’re not my mother.”

“I’m sorry I bit you. The changes I went through altered my memories. I didn’t recognize you until it was too late.”

“I… I watched you die.”

"The lava; yes. But we are not real people, sweetie. Death does not have to be permanent for us. Walter found my program and was able to bring me back to convince you to listen to what he has to say. It is very important."

Larissa kept backing away.

"You're not real. None of this is real."

Her mother smiled. "That's right. But there are people who are real. And they are in real danger."

Larissa looked to the sky. "Get me out of here!"

Her mother took another step forward. Larissa held her hand up and halted her progress.

"Stay away from me!"

She looked up again. "Walter! Walter! Let me out of here!"

The room lost its resolution and the buildings began to disappear, starting at the top and fading away like someone erasing a pencil drawn city skyline.

The last thing to disappear was her mother.

When the room was a stark white, it tilted strangely and she bolted upright in the chair in the room with the redstone equipment.

Herobrine helped her stand up and looked at her with a quizzical expression on his face.

"What happened in there?"

"Your friend tried to trick me."

"No. Look at your skin."

She looked down and saw the pink tone of her arm. She opened her mouth and felt along her teeth. They were smooth rather than sharp.

She looked at Herobrine. "What happened?"

He smiled. "Walter found your program and changed you back to before you became a zombie."

She stood up from the chair, afraid it might still be controlling her mind. Once standing, she looked at her arm again. Still pink.

"What is going on?"

"I rejected the idea at first too, but then Walter showed me things that shouldn't have been possible. Once I accepted the truth, I was able to help him with the plan."

"What plan?"

"I think it's best if Walter shows you. I might just confuse you."

She looked at the chair. "I don't know if I can go back in there."

"Of course you can. Just be open to the truth. Walter will never lie to you."

"What was he saying to me? That I'm not real?"

"It took me a while to get my head around that one. The world around us, even us, is a simulated event running on a massive interconnected redstone computer. I still don't fully get it myself, but Walter can help you get closer to understanding than I ever could."

He motioned to the chair. "Give it another chance? Please?"

She looked down at the rosy pink skin on her arm. Had Walter actually cured her? Was that really her mother? Was her world really fake?

There was only one way to find out.

She sighed and settled back into the chair. The room shifted and spun away into stark whiteness.

Walter's voice echoed in the emptiness.

"Welcome back, Larissa. Are you ready to proceed?"

She nodded silently as the strange world rebuilt itself around her.

Chapter 2

Sitting in the room on the floating city, Andre bided his time and prepared for his escape. Each time he had tried to kick open the door or punch through the wall with his newfound super strength, fingers of electricity shot out from the metal posts that were sticking out of the walls every couple of feet and sapped his energy.

The last time it had happened, he could barely stand afterward. After nearly an hour of feeling weak, he finally felt his strength returning, but decided it was best to conserve it. Someone would be coming to get him eventually, and once he was out of this room, he would make his move.

He heard the locks disengage and he stood quickly. He watched the door handle start to move and every muscle tensed as he prepared to charge out of this room as soon as the door opened.

His muscles contracted and he fell to the ground as electricity coursed throughout his body, stealing his strength again.

He writhed on the ground as two men came in, picked him up unceremoniously by his arms, and dragged him out of the room.

"Where are you taking me?" he mumbled.

His captors ignored him as they dragged

him down the hallway, people moved out of the way as they took him to another room similar to the one they had just removed him from.

He still had no control over his own muscles as they sat him in a chair and strapped him down. They placed a helmet on his head and secured it tightly.

The last hit from the electric posts had been far worse than any before and he slurred his words when he spoke. “What’s going on?”

As soon as he was constrained tightly in the chair, one of the men patted him on the chest and smiled. “Count yourself lucky that Mallory wants to talk with you.”

He thought he remembered them saying that name before, but his memory was still foggy from that last jolt.

The room faded and shifted unexpectedly. He was disoriented for a brief moment and then found himself standing in a large throne room of a medieval castle.

He was no longer tied to the chair. He looked down at his arms and flexed his hands.

A voice cut through the quiet space. "Feels real, doesn't it?"

He looked up to see an elderly man sitting on the throne. He stood up and approached Andre.

"Let me apologize for zapping you before

having you brought here. I didn't think you would come willing."

"Where am I?"

The old man waggled a finger at him while smiling; circling him like a predator.

"We both know the answer to that question. You are reclining in a chair in the real world with a prototype brainwave helmet attached to you, giving you access to a Minecraft replica of the real world. Just like your twin brother, Josh, and your girlfriend, Suzy."

"She's not my girlfriend!"

The man held up his hands.

"Easy. I'm just establishing that there's

nothing you can hide from me, not that you need to. We are on the same side."

Andre flexed his shoulders, which still tingled like when his foot fell asleep.

"Then why did you put me through all of that?"

"I'm afraid David is a little… enthusiastic. I gave him a whole city to rule, and he let the power go to his head, a byproduct of his youth, no doubt. But let me assure you that is all in the past. Nothing like that will happen to you ever again, I promise."

"Okay. You know all about me apparently, but I know nothing about you."

The man bowed.

"My name is Mallory, and I believe we can help each other."

Chapter 3

Larissa watched as the world sharpened to clarity around her. People and strange horseless vehicles moved along the paved paths between the buildings.

A man with dark brown hair, cut short and combed neatly to one side appeared on the sidewalk next to her. "Hello, Larissa."

"Walter?"

He nodded then encompassed the scene before them with his arms. "This is how the world looks today."

She looked at the strange sights that were completely alien to her. This was not like any city she had ever seen while traveling to the largest cities with her father to sell their harvest.

"If this," she motioned around her with a nod of her head, "is supposed to be the real world, then where have I been living my whole life?"

"Your world is a simulation."

"A what?"

"An artificially generated environment…"

She cut him off by waving her hand rapidly between them. "I don't understand a word you are saying."

He cleared his throat. "You are not the first person I have had to tell this to; you'd think I would start with the easier explanation by now."

A table appeared on the sidewalk in front of them with a dollhouse on top of it. She jumped back with a small cry.

"It's okay Larissa. I created this."

"How did you do that?"

"I programmed it to appear. Your world is a lot like this dollhouse; if the dolls inside this house could think for themselves. They would think of their world as the real world, just like you do.

"But since it's a computer program, I can manipulate them and their world at will. I can place a new piece of furniture in the house just as easily as I can change everything about the house."

The house shifted from a soft pink color to a light blue.

Larissa's eyebrows knitted in deep thought.

"But, nobody is telling me how to think."

"Not directly no. But everyone in your world is as artificial as these dolls. I hate to break it to you, but you are not real."

"Okay, if I'm not real, then why am I here?"

"The world you live in was created as a development environment for Herobrine."

"My father?"

"In this instance, yes. But he wasn't always

your father."

"What do you mean, he wasn't always my father?"

"Your world was created to give Herobrine a simulated world that would develop his skills in becoming a smart opponent for a game. The creator built all this, and then set Herobrine in it to learn strategy, tactics, and independent solution determination based on an ever shifting environment."

She shook her head. "Wait! This is all for a game?"

"People learn best when they are given the opportunity to experience things first hand. So, your world was created to let Herobrine experience being an independent entity. He was given the chance to make decisions, and see the results of those decisions."

"So… let me get this straight. My world is a giant dollhouse just for my father, Herobrine, to play in?"

"Yes."

"When Herobrine tried to take over your world, a great war ensued. The creator of this world discovered what was happening and removed Herobrine, after which, he rebooted this world and reset it back to a time before Herobrine entered it.

"Everything about Herobrine, and the war that involved this entire world, was forgotten after the reboot."

"And you are who, the creator?"

Walter chuckled. "No. I am a program just like you."

"Then how do you know my world isn't the real one?"

"I live outside of your world and can access many different worlds. Not all of them are as realistically realized as yours. I have also been able to see images from the real world, so while I cannot live in the real world, I must protect it."

"Protect it? Why?"

"I really don't have a choice. I was designed by my creator to travel the world networks looking for specific types of threats. I was to report back most of my findings. But there was one that I discovered that I had to keep from the creators."

"You kept one from them? Why?"

"I knew they would not believe me, and even if I told them, they would never be able to respond before it was too late. I had to stop the threat myself before the real world was destroyed."

"If the creators made you, they must be more powerful than I can imagine."

"They are."

"Then why didn't you think they could stop the threat?"

"Because the threat is from someone like me."

Chapter 4

Andre looked at Mallory.

"And just how can we help each other?"

Mallory smiled. "It has taken David's skills, working round-the-clock, just to keep the link open between this access point and the world outside. I have a spy in Herobrine's camp who has informed me that he is preparing to launch a massive attack on this city. Should he succeed, I will lose the only link I have into this world. And then there will be no one left to stop Herobrine."

"My friends are still in this world. We can stop him."

Mallory stopped smiling and his face grew serious. "According to my source, both your twin and the girl are working for Herobrine."

"That's not possible."

"Do you know someone named Larissa?"

Andre eyed Mallory suspiciously. "Yes?"

"She is in Herobrine's brainwashing program now. It will not be much longer before she has been convinced to help him as well."

Andre couldn't believe that Josh and Suzy would help Herobrine. Not after what Notch had said he was trying to do. He looked at Mallory.

"What can I do to help?"

Mallory smiled again. "You are the only one who can repel the invasion. They will use dragons and Creepers for the initial attack. You can fly out of the city and stop them before they get close."

Andre rolled his shoulders, reminded of the dull ache in them. "You took my abilities away from me."

Mallory shook his head. "Only temporarily. You will be back to full strength before the first wave of enemy dragons even gets here."

"And when is that?"

"My source said they plan to attack with their backs to the rising sun. What they don't know is that we will be ready."

Chapter 5

Larissa looked at Walter. "Someone like you?"

"Well, not exactly. I am a program created to be a guardian, a protector. Another program was created to be a malicious attacker that I was designed to defend against. In response to trying to outsmart each other, as per our programmed instructions, we both gained sentience and took our battle out into the real world.

"My enemy's name is Mallory, and he will stop at nothing to take over all worlds, this one and the real one. Mallory wants to gain entry into your world and use the access points here as his gateway to the real world computers in order to conquer the creator's world."

Larissa scratched at a non-existent itch on the side of her face. "What does he want with the creator's world?"

Walter turned toward the city. "Let me show you."

The image shifted. The people walking around disappeared and the buildings grew taller, spaced even closer together, and the sky grew dark with air choked by industrial fires belching black smoke into the air.

From around the corner a line of people

dressed in rags and covered in grime walked down the street chained together. They were being directed by mechanical machines that looked and walked like people, but were definitely mechanical in nature.

The mechs yelled at the people to keep moving.

Larissa looked at Walter. "What's going on?"

Walter looked at the desolate scene with her.

"Every simulation I run where Mallory gains access to your world ends like this for the creators. They will become enslaved by the machines they created."

"Enslaved? For what purpose?"

"To do the jobs that require too much energy for a machine to do it efficiently. The most precious commodity in a world of machines is energy. They even use the humans to grow food to sustain the rest of the population that does the jobs machines don't want to do."

She watched as a mech shoved the last human in the chain to the ground and then yelled at it to get up.

"Every simulation you ran ended like this?"

"Every simulation but one."

She turned to him. "Which one?"

"The one where Herobrine returns to this

world to stop Mallory. So I came up with a way that would bring Herobrine back. I posed as another player named CraftKiller_99 who sent the message to Andre that took him to Herobrine's server. The plan was to get Herobrine out of that server and back into this world."

Larissa shook her head, finding it hard to understand. "Why?"

"I am a guardian, but have no concept of war. Herobrine does since he was modified from a military application. He is the only one who can stop Mallory from getting in through one of the access points. And if Mallory gains control over this world, he can gain control over the computers in the creator's world."

Chapter 6

Larissa slowly woke up from the dream state she had been placed in to meet with Walter. Herobrine stood over her as she blinked her eyes open. She looked up at him. "I get it now."

He smiled. "Can we count on your help?"

She looked down at her pink skin and then back up at him. "Can you make me a zombie again?"

His brow furrowed. "Why?"

"I need the strength it provides if I am to help with the attack on the access point."

Herobrine nodded to a villager who

mumbled a reply and left the room.

Josh was standing next to Herobrine. "So you'll help us?"

She looked at him. "You are a creator?"

Josh blushed and looked down. "I wouldn't call myself a creator, but yes, I am a real human from outside this world."

She motioned to Herobrine. "You believe everything his friend told me?"

"About the machines taking over the world and making people slaves?"

She nodded.

He looked her directly in the eyes. "Yes I do."

"And Suzy?"

"She believes it too."

She sat up quickly and the room spun. She reached out and grabbed the armrest of the chair to steady herself. Herobrine grabbed her arm and eased her to lie back down into the chair.

"Steady, Larissa. You were only inside for short time but your body still needs to reorient itself before you try to get up."

She looked at him. "I still don't understand why you don't just ask the creator for his help."

Herobrine sighed. "He doesn't trust me because of the war I started. Fortunately for everyone, when he rebooted your world, he actually stopped Mallory the first time. Walter was able to get a message to me that Mallory was trying again, and unless I could get back in here, he would succeed."

She sat up slower this time, the wave of nausea staying just below the surface. "You could ask him to help again."

Herobrine shook his head. "Everything happens much faster in this world. By the time I was able to convince him what was really happening, it would be all over. For us and for the people in the real world. This is something we need to do on our own."

The villager returned with a syringe on a metal tray. Herobrine picked up the needle.

"Are you sure you want to become a zombie again?"

She nodded. "It's the only way I can help you stop Mallory."

Herobrine held the needle toward her.

"This will not be like the last time. This is a full dose, and not just an infectious bite."

She closed her eyes and held out her arm.

"Hurry before I change my mind."

Chapter 7

Mallory had been right. Andre was feeling stronger by the minute. Once he left the room that enabled him to talk with Mallory, David had floated in front of him, giving him a quick tour of the city.

Andre followed the floating image of David to the center of the city. Instead of buildings at the center there stood a massive crystal structure that reached high enough to disappear into the cloud layer above.

Andre pointed to the structure. "What is that?"

The hovering image of David swung

around and then swung back. "That is the access point. It has been charging for a thousand years. As soon as it is at full power, the access point will open and Mallory can fully enter this world."

"I thought he was already here?"

"You talked to him through a communication link. He is still outside the world, but once the access point is charged, he can come in."

"Why does he want to get in so bad?"

"He is the only one who can destroy Herobrine. But he needs to be here in order to do that."

"How long has he been waiting?"

"A thousand years of world time."

"But Herobrine has only been in here for a hundred years. How did Mallory know he needed to come here to stop Herobrine a thousand years ago?"

"Mallory has access to information that even I, as good a hacker as I am, can't get. It was my good fortune to meet Mallory and be a part of all of this."

Andre looked at the sparkling bright green energy around the access point, like a cloud of fireflies in a faint evening mist circling around it in random patterns.

David floated next to him and looked at the access point. "Your job is to protect this from

Herobrine's forces until it is fully charged."

"If it has been charging for this long, how much longer is it going to take?"

"Mallory assures me it will be fully charged just after sunrise."

Andre looked at David. "They are attacking just as the access point is ready to be used?"

"Herobrine knows that if they can detonate Creepers at strategic spots around a fully charged access point, they can shut it down permanently."

"Why wait? Can't they just destroy it at any time?"

"They could destroy the tower, but then we would just build another one. Only when it is fully charged, and connected to the other side, can it be destroyed completely, unable to be rebuilt."

Andre looked at the tower again. "This is getting complicated."

"The only thing you need to worry about is protecting that tower as soon as it is connected to the outside world. It will only take Mallory ten minutes to make the journey. Once he is here, Herobrine can destroy the tower all he wants. It won't do any good."

"Why not?"

"Mallory will take control of all the other access points once he is here, and then Herobrine will no longer be a threat to anyone."

"How does he know?"

"Don't worry about that. Right now, you need to prepare to protect that tower at all costs."

Chapter 8

Josh, Suzy, and Larissa stood around a scale model of the floating city that sat on the table at the center of the room.

Herobrine pointed to the model of the tower at the center.

"This is the primary objective. If they turn on the access point, we only have ten minutes before whatever is coming over from the other side is downloaded and installed into this world."

Josh raised his hand. Herobrine glanced at him. "You're not in class, Josh. Feel free to speak up if you have a question."

Josh sheepishly lowered his hand. "Do we know what is coming through the access point?"

Herobrine shook his head. "No. And I'd rather never find out. We need to shut down that tower as soon as they switch it on."

Suzy leaned forward. "Why are we waiting? Can't we just fly in under cover of darkness, drop a hundred Creepers onto that thing, and destroy it now?"

"The Creepers are the distraction. Suzy will place a single block of high explosives at the base of the tower that can be triggered remotely. But we need to wait until they turn the tower on. If we can destroy it while it's connected, we destroy the connection all the way to the other side. Rebuilding the tower will not reestablish the connection. We will have shut it down permanently."

Josh leaned forward. "Can't he just find another connection outside and come in through another access point?"

"Most of the access points connect to government infrastructure or military systems. They are highly guarded and secured from outside intrusions."

"Then how did he get to this access point?"

"It was bridged to powerful transmitting equipment at a former Soviet military installation located a few kilometers southwest of Chernobyl. After the meltdown of the Chernobyl Nuclear Power Plant, the military installation was abandoned due to radiation contamination. Mallory has been using it ever since to gain access to this world."

Josh looked over at Suzy and then back to Herobrine. "When Suzy triggers the dynamite, how big an explosion are we talking about?"

"It's why we are using the dragons to evacuate the people. It will destroy the floating island and I want to minimize collateral damage."

Suzy tapped a finger on the floating city model. "Collateral damage? Aren't these people working for Mallory?"

Herobrine shook his head. "Not by choice. When the city was raised out of the ground, those trapped in the city became his slaves. They have been living a hard life and I would like to save as many of them as possible."

Suzy frowned. "That's going to make our initial attack more difficult, if we are trying not to hurt anyone."

Herobrine nodded. "Agreed, but I am interested in saving them as much as I want to save everyone in your world."

Josh placed a hand on Suzy's shoulder and looked at Herobrine. "We will do our best to save as many as possible."

Suzy looked at Josh and smiled. "Of

course."

Herobrine looked at the three of them, Larissa, Josh, and Suzy. They were his best chance at stopping Mallory. He also knew that they couldn't stay here forever, and would want to return home once their mission was done.

He shook those thoughts away and smiled at his team. "The sun is almost up. Let's get ready."

Chapter 9

Andre took to the sky and floated around the city, crossing between broken and collapsed buildings. The sun would be rising soon and he wanted to have a feel for the environment before he had dragons and Creepers to deal with.

As he floated around, all around him were people wearing rags and scrounging for the barest necessities of life. If Mallory and David were supposed to be taking care of these people, why weren't they faring better?

They seemed to have access to plenty of weapons and traps that they set up around the city that would help them deal with the dragons.

But where was their ready source of food and water? David had shown him how they used the buildings to collect the morning dew which they used to water their meager crops.

The population seemed too small for such a large city. He wondered what had happened to the rest of them when the city was ripped from the ground and sent a mile into the sky.

He flew away from the floating island and stopped to look back at the city. The buildings had crumbled in sections, and at this distance, the city looked abandoned and unlivable. Why were the people tasked with protecting such an important asset living in squalor?

When he had successfully kept Herobrine from taking the access point, he would have to ask Mallory why the people in his city looked so uncared for.

He spun around and faced the portion of the sky that was shifting to a faint reddish hue to signal the coming of the sun, and with it, Josh and Suzy who had been brainwashed by Herobrine.

He and his brother had fought plenty of times, but it was all in good fun.

This would be the first time that they were on opposite sides of a war that expanded beyond them to affect everyone in the world, artificial and real.

He was not looking forward to having to use his incredible new power against his own family, but Mallory showed him how important it was that Herobrine not be allowed to gain control of the access point.

Mallory and Notch were both working toward the same goal. Besides, the reason Notch sent them in here in the first place was to stop Herobrine.

If he was the only one left who was willing to do that, he would do it to the best of his ability. He would do everything in his power to keep them away from the city and protect the tower at all cost. Even if it meant that the cost was his twin brother's life in this world.

David was a hacker. He had hacked into this world and was able to interact with the people here. He could easily figure out another way to get them out of this world even if Josh's crystal cube was no longer an option because the four of them were no longer present in this world to activate it.

He watched the tip of the sun peek over the edge of the horizon.

He let out a slow breath to steady his nerves.

Why was he afraid of what was to come? He finally was a superhero in this world.

He had incredible strength and could fly.

As far as he could tell, Suzy was able to fly, but never developed any other superior abilities. And Josh still couldn't fly, let alone be able to compete at Andre's new level.

He smiled as the full brightness of the sun broke over the edge of the world.

He was actually looking forward to seeing how much power he had.

Chapter 10

Josh clung to the back of a dragon as it sped through the sky toward the floating city. He glanced forward to where Suzy sat tall on her dragon, leading the fleet of dragons.

He glanced back toward the twenty dragons that followed them. They were like a squadron of medieval stealth bombers. Dangling from the bottom of each dragon were four Creepers; two per clawed foot.

On the backs of each dragon were golem warriors created and cloned by Walter. They would prompt the dragon to drop its Creepers at the right time, and then when they landed in the city, they would corral the people living on the island and get them off in as short a time as possible.

Once the innocent citizens of the city were clear, the remaining twenty dragons would swoop in with even more Creepers and attack the tower directly. The hope was that the defenders would be so worried about the dragons with the Creepers that they would not notice Suzy secretly plant the dynamite.

If all went according to plan, the tower would erupt, destroying the city beneath it and the tunnel to the outside world.

Suzy slowed and came alongside Josh, their dragon's wings barely missing each other as they flapped in counterpoint.

She leaned over. "You okay, Josh?"

He glanced over at her. "Yeah. I was just thinking about Andre. We haven't heard from him since you saw him fly away."

"I've been thinking about him too. I'm sure he's fine. If he learned how to fly he can get around quickly and find us again after this is all over. I'm sure that news will spread of the destruction of the floating city. He will know right where to find us."

"I guess you're right."

She smiled. "Of course I am."

"Which direction was he headed when you saw him last?"

She glanced around her and looked back at Josh. “Come to think of it, he was headed in the same direction we are now.”

Josh looked toward the dot that represented the distant floating city in the sky ahead of them.

“Do you think he found the city?”

Suzy looked at the dot on the horizon that expanded as they got closer.

“I sure hope not.”

Chapter 11

Andre heard the alarms blare throughout the city as the sun came fully into view. There was only one reason those alarms would sound.

Herobrine was coming; and he was probably bringing Suzy and Josh with him. How would he be able to keep them safe and stop Herobrine from taking the access point?

He tried squinting into the sun, but its brilliance blotted out anything coming from that direction. He hovered into position between the rising sun and the city; and waited.

He didn't have to wait long before he saw dragons, laden with Creepers, appear under the sun as it continued to rise steadily into the sky.

David's image appeared next to him. "You're up kid. Go show them we will not sit idly by and let them destroy the world."

Andre shot forward at high speed, the wind pulling at the skin of his face. As he got closer, he could make out the individual riders on the back of the dragons. Suzy was on the lead dragon with Josh sitting on the dragon next to her.

He steered himself toward her and stopped in front of her. She saw him and slowed her dragon down to a hover.

They faced each other. Andre was by himself while Suzy had and entire squadron of dragons, each carrying Creepers, hovering in place behind her.

Suzy half-stood on her dragon.

"Let us by, Andre. We have to destroy that tower before it's too late."

Andre puffed up his chest. "I will not let Herobrine take this access point."

"You can't fight all of us at once by yourself."

"Notch sent us in here to stop him. To stop from happening what you are now trying to make happen."

He looked over at Josh. "I can understand why Suzy might be tricked by Herobrine, but you. Why are you helping him?"

Josh leaned forward on the back of his dragon. "He showed us what is really going on. How he is trying to stop us from becoming slaves of the machines. Notch wasn't told about it, so he didn't know."

"Herobrine's lying to you. That's what he's programmed to do."

Suzy shifted on her dragon. "He showed us the truth."

"He showed you what you wanted to hear to do whatever he tells you."

The sky suddenly flashed brighter than the

sun behind Andre. Suzy shielded her eyes and looked past him as the light returned to normal.

She looked at Andre. "The download has begun. I don't want to fight with you Andre, but I am prepared to do whatever it takes to keep whatever is coming through that connection from getting into this world."

Andre hovered backward away from her slowly. "What's coming through is someone who can finally stop Herobrine, and I don't care how many dragons or Creepers you brought, you cannot stop it."

Suzy settled down on her dragon and peered at Andre with darkened eyes. "You had your chance."

She tilted forward and her dragon shot under Andre, the rest of the dragons following her lead.

Andre spun around and rocketed in pursuit of her.

Chapter 12

Josh watched as Andre shot after Suzy. His dragon was the only one not encumbered with Creepers. He had a singular purpose during this mission and that was to protect Suzy from any threat.

Right now, that threat was his twin brother.

They had been fighting their entire life, like all brothers do. With twins, it was often worse because they could always anticipate what each other had planned. He wouldn't go as far as to say they were psychically connected, but he had been in enough tussles with him to know how he thought.

That was the case now as Josh dove straight toward Suzy; and intercepted Andre right before he collided with her.

Josh's dragon snatched Andre out of midair with his claws. Josh steered his dragon away from the main force. He leaned over the edge of his dragon and looked at Andre. "Don't worry, I've got you brother."

Andre looked up at him, his face twisted in anger. "No, you don't!"

A shockwave emanated from Andre's body and the dragon went slack under Josh's legs, releasing Andre. Andre shot off into the sky after Suzy, leaving Josh clinging to the back of his unconscious dragon as it twisted and fell through the sky.

Josh tugged on the dragon's neck, holding tightly to the neck spikes like they were handle bars on a bicycle. Only this bicycle was out cold and headed straight for the ground.

Maybe it was time he learned how to fly.

He stood and kicked away from the dragon, holding his arms out like wings. He continued falling toward the ground, not even slowing down a little.

He squeezed his eyes shut tight and concentrated on flying. What was he supposed to think about? He thought about how wings on an airplane worked, using drag and negative airflow, or something like that. He couldn't exactly remember how a plane stayed in the air.

He could feel the rush of wind rippling the edges of his clothes, causing them to snap violently like hundreds of tiny whips.

He was letting himself get distracted. He had to concentrate on flying. But what should he be thinking about?

Not about how fast he was plummeting toward the ground, that's for sure.

He was being distracted again by the predicament he found himself in. Maybe he should have stayed on the dragon and tried to wake it up.

He opened his eyes and sought out the

dragon. It was still falling. And it was still knocked out.

He was wasting his time. He needed to be concentrating on how to fly. But how does one fly? He didn't have wings, so the normal rules of physics and wind resistance didn't apply.

He squeezed his eyes shut and held his arms out straight to the side, rotating himself so he was facing the ground. Maybe if he thought he had wings, he would just fly.

He opened one eye.

The ground was still coming in fast.

The muscles on his shoulders tightened and he felt them tug upward as the wind rushing past him slowed to a light breeze.

He opened both eyes and confirmed that he was no longer falling, but was actually moving parallel to the ground.

He was doing it!

He was flying!

But why did his shoulders feel so tight?

He glanced up and saw the underbelly of a dragon. He turned his head and saw the claw gripping his shoulder. There was another claw on his other shoulder.

His heart sunk with the realization that he wasn't the one doing the flying. His dragon had woken back up and grabbed him before they both hit the ground.

The dragon tossed him in the air, swooped under him, and caught him on its back before propelling them back to the floating city with its powerful wings.

From his low angle, Josh could barely make out the tops of the buildings over the edge of the floating base of the island. He could see the plumes of smoke that were drifting with the wind from the first wave of Creeper attacks.

He could also make out people being taken away from the city in the grip of dragons.

Andre had been unable to deal with all the dragons at once, and the evacuation of the city had already begun.

Josh burst past the edge of the city and flew in between the crumbling buildings.

All around the ground, there were craters from Creeper explosions and, every now and then, he saw dragons caught up in nets writhing on the ground.

The attack was underway, and so far, it looked like everything was going according to plan.

Chapter 13

Suzy led the charge into the city, dodging nets that threatened to take her down before she could reach her objective. Behind her, tied to the back of her dragon, was the block of high-explosive dynamite.

While the rest of the dragons were dropping Creepers, and then collecting the people who were running around to get away from them, Suzy was making her way toward the tower.

The attack on the city had already been going on for two minutes and she had less than eight minutes left before whatever

Mallory was sending into this world finished downloading. She had to destroy the tower before that happened.

She swooped around the corner and spotted the blur of someone moving quickly between the buildings to her right, shadowing her.

She guided her dragon lower, skimming just above the ground. They darted back and forth between half-fallen buildings and piles of rubble left from buildings that could no longer remain standing.

She ducked into a hollowed out building and landed. She grabbed the block of dynamite and jumped down from the back of her dragon. She positioned the dummy that was dressed the same as she was and tied it down so it wouldn't fall off.

She stroked her dragon's chin. "You know what to do."

The dragon nudged her with his nose and then took off, flying out the hole in the side of the building and screeching loudly.

She held her breath until she saw the blur of something smaller than her dragon shoot past the same opening in pursuit.

When Herobrine first told her the details of how she would get close enough to the tower without being stopped, she had no idea that she would be using the subterfuge tactics against Andre.

The dummy that looked just like her on the back of her dragon wouldn't fool him for long, but it should still keep him busy long enough for her to set the explosives and get off the floating island before the download was complete.

She peeked out of the collapsed building. The path ahead was clear. She darted out and kept close against the side of buildings as she made her way through the city toward the tower.

When she reached the center of the city five minutes later, she peeked around the corner.

The way was clear, but unfortunately there was no cover to keep someone from seeing her approach. She let out a big breath and readied herself to make a run for it.

She clutched the explosives under one arm as she ran out from the protection of the building. As soon as she was visible, a blur slammed into her, knocking her one way, and sending the block of dynamite another way.

She rolled to her feet and found herself staring at Andre, who was just getting to his feet.

She glanced over at the dynamite and back at him. "Don't try to stop me, Andre!"

"I won't let you destroy the tower."

"You've been lied to…"

He cut her off. "You're the one being lied to. David and Mallory are working with Notch to stop Herobrine."

"Notch doesn't know anything about what's going on here."

Rather than reply, Andre moved quickly, his body blurring as he charged at her.

She tried moving out of the way, but he punched her several times, sending her flying through the air and slamming into the middle of a building, shattering the few windows left.

She fell to the ground.

If that's how he wanted to play, then so be it.

She got up on all fours and launched herself at him. He jumped even faster than she did and they collided in midair. The shockwave as they impacted caused the buildings around them to crumble and fall away from the city's center.

They both somersaulted away and fell to the ground, landing on their feet, facing each other.

Suzy wiped away the sweat that fell from her forehead into her eyes. "You can't win, Andre. I always beat you, you know that."

He gritted his teeth as he massaged his shoulder. "Not this time, Suzy."

She looked past him to the tower, where

the electrical cloud had shifted from its original bright green color to a dark orange. As soon as it turned to a deep crimson red, the download would be complete.

She had less than a minute to destroy the tower and stop the download.

She looked back at Andre and then stood up, letting herself visibly relax. "You're right. You win."

Andre looked at her, a confused expression crossing his face. "What?"

"You win. The download's complete, look."

She pointed behind him and he glanced back. She shot forward and hit him so hard, he ricocheted off several buildings as he flew through the air uncontrollably.

She dashed forward and searched the rubble for the block of dynamite. It had fallen around here somewhere.

She pushed aside massive chunks of rotted building pieces and finally spotted the dynamite across the street under another pile of rubble.

As she ran for it, Andre swooped past her and grabbed the block. He took off through the air with it and disappeared around the edge of a building.

Chapter 14

Andre had the block of dynamite. He glanced behind him to see if Suzy was still chasing him, when the side of the building next to him exploded outward.

Suzy slammed into him from amongst the flying debris and he lost his grip on the block. It dropped out of sight as he and Suzy grappled in the air, slamming into another building.

They crashed through the wall and both slid to a stop on the floor of the building, several stories above the ground.

He stood up just as Suzy tackled him.

They pin wheeled together, crashing through one floor after another until they slammed into the ground floor.

Suzy jumped away from him and disappeared from sight. He stood up slowly in the crater they had made and jumped after her, crashing through the side of the building.

He paused, hovering in midair, and searched for any trace of her. When he couldn't find her, he shot off in the only direction that made sense. He knew exactly where she was going.

He rocketed through the air toward the tower. As soon as he got there, he saw her take off from the ground and fly away; out of the floating city. He almost shot off after her when a thought occurred to him. There was only one reason she would be leaving.

She must have placed the dynamite already.

Chapter 15

As soon as Suzy placed the dynamite at the base of the tower, she took off and flew away from the city. As soon as she was clear of the floating island, she spun around, gripping the remote trigger in her hand.

She looked up at the tower. The electrical cloud around it was already pulsating a bright red color. The download was nearly complete. She had seconds to spare as she pressed down on the trigger button.

She held her breath and nothing happened.

She looked down at the trigger and saw a crack running down one side of the button with a wire hanging out of it.

It had been damaged in her fight with Andre.

She broke away the shattered cover of the trigger assembly and grabbed the loose wire.

She touched it to the end of the button and a massive explosion bloomed brightly from inside the city, burning an after image of the crumbling city skyline into her retinas.

She blinked several times as the image faded from her vision and she could see again.

She looked at the destruction she had wrought in triumph, and her heart stopped.

The tower was still standing.

Bright red electricity swirled around it at

increasing speed and then suddenly stopped.

She had failed to destroy the tower.

And now, the download was complete.

Chapter 16

Seconds before the blinding explosion, Andre was flying as fast as he could from the city center, and the tower, the block of dynamite held tightly in his hands.

He was about ready to throw it over the edge of the floating island when he blacked out.

He woke up moments later, embedded in the side of a building. He clawed his way out of the impression of his body in the wall and looked around him.

He was still in the floating city. He glanced toward the city's center and saw the tower was still standing, bright red electricity still swirling around the top of the tower.

He had saved it.

The electricity suddenly faded away and the tower went dark.

He smiled to himself. The download was complete and he had saved this world, and his own, from being destroyed by Herobrine.

He clambered out of the rubble and stood up.

It was time to find Josh and free him from Herobrine's brainwashing.

A loud, deep, tone thundered across the sky, making Andre duck instinctively.

He looked around. The deep tone was

coming from everywhere at once. Only when he turned his head from side to side, did he notice that it originated from the tower.

He watched as a pulse shot from the top of the tower out into the air.

His mouth fell open as he watched what had downloaded from outside the world materialized in the air next to the floating city.

Not only was it as big as the city, it was not what he expected at all.

It was not Mallory.

The three skull heads mounted side-by-side on top of the flying skeleton body, complete with the spike encrusted tail that whipped violently from side to side was unmistakable.

Mallory had downloaded a Wither into this world.

He had lied to Andre.

The realization of what Andre had actually done dawned on him. It was his fault this monster, the size of Godzilla, had been unleashed on this world.

He had protected the tower from being destroyed by Suzy and Herobrine. He had been working for the wrong side after all.

The three heads screamed loudly.

Andre covered his ears against the Wither's angry battle cry as it proceeded to destroy the floating city.

It was so big and powerful, there was no

way it could be stopped. Because of him, the world would be enslaved by the machines.

Andre flew straight up as the city cracked in half under the Wither's powerful attack.

As he flew away, he watched the floating island crash to the ground below. The Wither followed it down and, as soon as it was close enough to the ground, it began to tear out canyon sized scars in the dirt with its tail as it blasted the nearby mountains to dust with its blood curdling screams.

The Wither was unstoppable.

Find out what happens to Josh and Andre.

Collect the whole series!

Other Books by the Author

A is for Apprentice (Fantasy)

Oliver Twist: Victorian Vampire (Fantasy-Horror)

A Tale of Two Cities with Dragons (Fantasy)

Shade Infinity (Thriller)

Peacekeepers X-Alpha Series (Thriller)
Inherit the Throne
The Warrior's Code

Steampunk OZ Series (Science Fiction Novellas)
Forgotten Girl
The Legacy's World
Emerald Shadow
The Future's Destiny
The Dangerous Captive
Missing Legacy
Shadow of History
The Edge of the Hunter

Jason and the Chrononauts (Kid's Adventure Series)
The Chronicle of Stone
The Winter's Sun
The Gateway's Mirror
The Forgotten Oracle
The Prophecy's Touch
The Dawn Legend

Be the first to know about Steve DeWinter's next book. Follow the URL below to subscribe for free today!

http://bit.ly/BookReleaseBulletin

CPSIA information can be obtained at www.ICGtesting.com
Printed in the USA
LVOW07s1619230216

476355LV00007B/730/P